Gerbil Mottos

The Night Is Short: Keep Busy

Always Keep Your Whiskers Clean

Celery Tops Come To Those Who Wait

Gerbil Mottos

Many Paws Make Quick Work

Curl Up Nose To Toes

Gerbil, (un)curled

Alison Hughes

Illustrations by

Suzanne Del Rizzo

Fitzhenry & Whiteside

Published in Canada by Fitzhenry & Whiteside, 195 Allstate Parkway, Markham, Ontario L3R 4T8

Published in the United States by Fitzhenry & Whiteside, 311 Washington Street, Brighton, Massachusetts 02135

www.fitzhenry.ca godwit@fitzhenry.ca

10 9 8 7 6 5 4 3 2 1

Library and Archives Canada Cataloguing in Publication
Hughes, Alison, 1966-, author
Gerbil, uncurled / Alison Hughes ; illustrations by Suzanne Del Rizzo.

Issued in print and electronic formats.
ISBN 978-1-55455-332-7 (bound).--ISBN 978-1-55455-828-5 (pdf)

I. Del Rizzo, Suzanne, illustrator II. Title.

PS8615.U3165G47 2015 jC813'.6 C2014-907185-X
C2014-907186-8

Publisher Cataloging-in-Publication Data (U.S)
ISBN: 978-1-55455-332-7 (bound)
Data available on file

Fitzhenry & Whiteside acknowledges with thanks the Canada Council for the Arts, and the Ontario Arts Council for their support of our publishing program.
We acknowledge the financial support of the Government of Canada through the Canada Book Fund (CBF) for our publishing activities.

Canada Council for the Arts
Conseil des Arts du Canada

Cover and interior design by Daniel Choi
Cover image by Suzanne Del Rizzo
Photography by Heather Hogan
Printed in Canada by Sheck Wah Tong Printing Press Ltd.

For my nieces and nephews
(and for Chocolate and Muffin, the busiest gerbils I ever knew).

–Alison Hughes

For my parents, Ann and Sam Crabbe, and Giampiero's parents, Teresa and Francesco Del Rizzo.

Through your stories, hugs, laughter, and your gentle ways, the love of Granin, Bampa, Nonna, and Nonno will always shine bright in my children's hearts.

–Suzanne Del Rizzo

"In a *ball*," Grandpa Gerbil squeaked, his little paws sketching a circle in the air. "*That's* how gerbils sleep. Curled up in a BALL. Just like it says in the Gerbil Mottos. Remember?"

"Nose To Toes." Little Gerbil nodded miserably. "I remember."

All gerbils learned the Gerbil Mottos.

Little Gerbil slept differently. She loved to stretch out in the sun. The more she tried to curl up, the more her body wanted to uncurl.

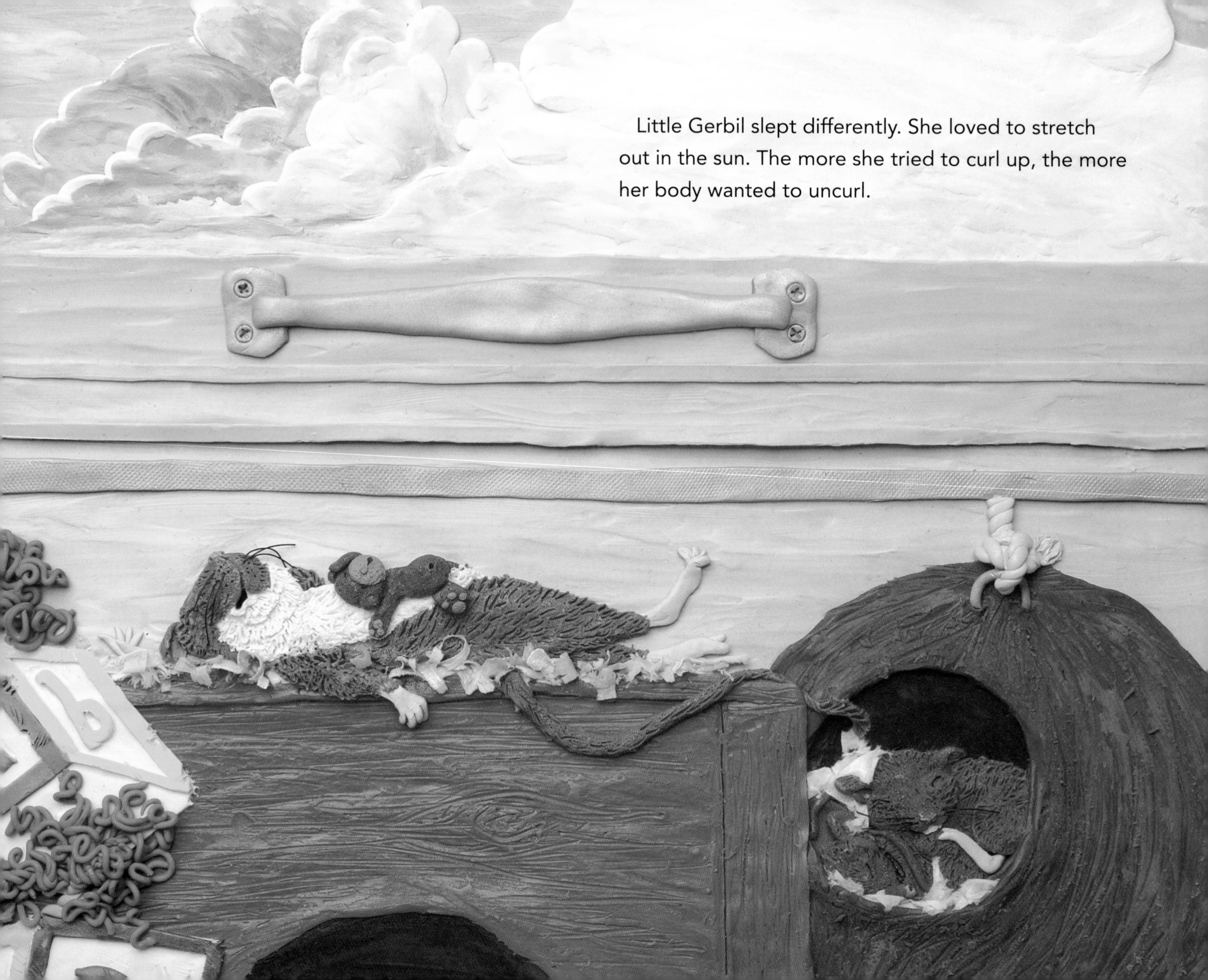

It started with a stretch in her tiniest gerbil toe.

The toe-stretch felt so good that her paw joined in...

...then her other paws, then her legs.
Soon, her whole body sttttrrreeettttched out.

Only then could she slip into a deep,
twitchless sleep.

But Little Gerbil listened to Grandpa Gerbil. He was kind and wise and five whole years old. A gerbil learns a lot in five years.

"I'll try, Grandpa Gerbil," Little Gerbil promised.

"Attagirl," he said. "Tail tucked in, and…"

"…nose to toes," finished Little Gerbil.

That morning, Little Gerbil curled up with her family under the bedding. She shut her eyes, tucked her nose into her toes, and wrapped her long tail around her body.

Relax, she thought. *It's nice and cozy down here. Snug. Very snug. And warm. Very, very warm...*

Little Gerbil panicked.

Too snug!

Too warm!

She couldn't breathe!

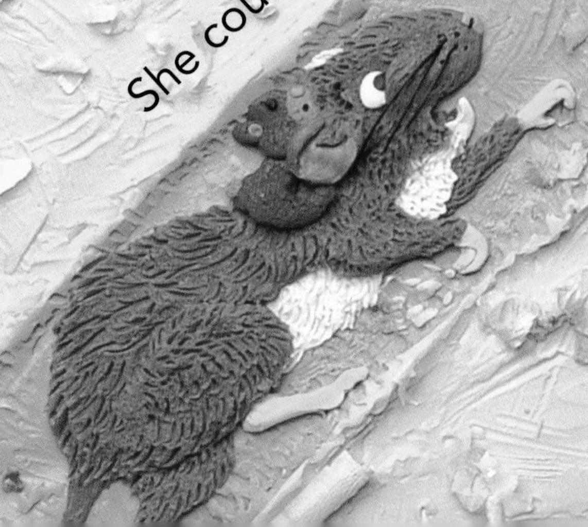

She poked her head up above the bedding and gulped fresh air.

Ahhhh. Better.

She thought of how lovely it would be to stretch out in the sunshine. But she remembered her promise, and sank back down among the sleeping gerbils.

Little Gerbil lay awake in the dark, cramped into a little ball, and waited for the day to end.

It was evening when Little Gerbil woke. She was on top of the bedding, on top of all the other gerbils, stretched out as flat as a pancake! She twitched, scratched, and remembered.

She had not slept curled up in a ball! She scrambled underneath the bedding, and huddled with the others. When her family woke, they congratulated Little Gerbil on curling up like a good gerbil. They gave her the biggest sunflower seed and the first scamper in the wheel.

Morning after morning, Little Gerbil tried to sleep gerbil-style.

But evening after evening, she awoke stretched out up top,

and scurried under the bedding before the others woke up.

Little Gerbil was miserable. She was living a gerbil lie.

Oh nuts and seeds, she thought, *I have to tell somebody.*

She found Mama Gerbil scampering in the wheel.

"Can't…squeak…now," she panted. "Must…keep…busy…."

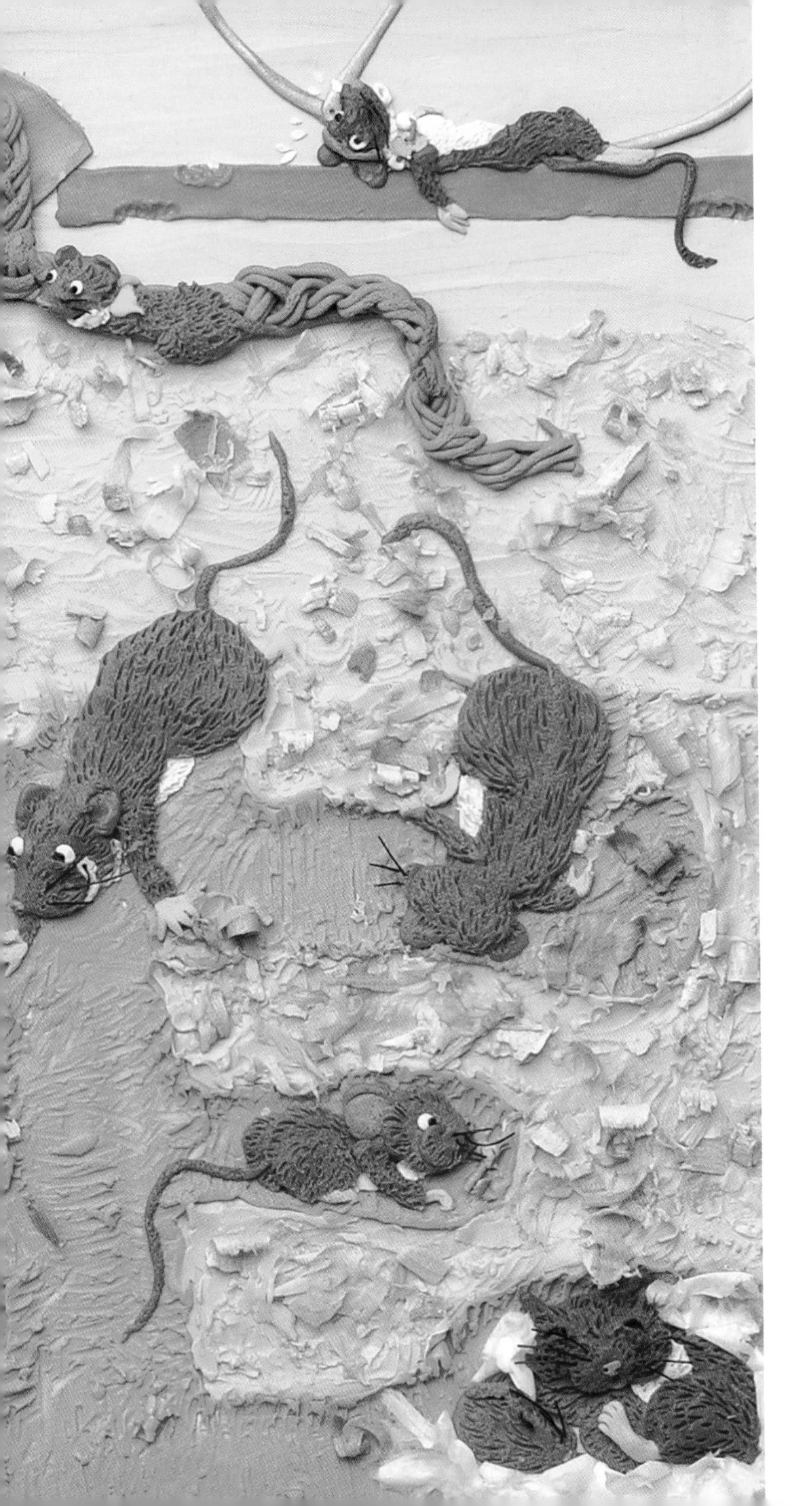

Little Gerbil sighed and sank down in the wood chips, paws covering her head. She listened to her busy family's chattering and scurrying. She heard the rhythmic thumping of the wheel stop and Mama Gerbil sigh. She saw her sister scrub her fuzzy whiskers, look around, and scrub them again. She saw Grandma Gerbil yawn and Grandpa Gerbil stretch stiffly.

Little Gerbil thought all night while she kept busy digging new tunnels with the others. By the time it was almost morning, she had a plan.

Just before bedtime, all the gerbils gathered for Gerbil Circle, their weekly meeting. Little Gerbil hopped forward.

"I want to squeak about the Gerbil Mottos," she said in a trembling little voice.

The gerbils twitched nervously. This was big. The Mottos were almost never squeaked about. They just were.

"I can only sleep stretched out," Little Gerbil blurted, her tiny heart thumping. "I've only been pretending to sleep Nose to Toes. That Motto does not fit me. I don't fit it."

A circle of beady eyes stared at Little Gerbil.

"And after watching all of you, I don't think I'm the only gerbil who doesn't fit."

There was a long, twitchless silence.

Finally, Mama Gerbil sat up.

"Little Gerbil's right. I've tried to hide it," she admitted, "but sometimes I'd rather rest than keep busy."

Sister Gerbil sat up, her dusty whiskers glinting in the sun.

"No matter how hard I scrub," she squeaked sadly, "my whiskers will not stay clean."

The gerbils erupted in chatter. Every gerbil seemed to have something to squeak.

Grandpa Gerbil cleared his throat. The gerbils fell silent.

"I admit that sometimes, possibly, older gerbils might find it hard to stay as busy or curl up as tightly as they used to," he said.

Grandma Gerbil nodded.

"I've seen lots of changes in my life," Grandpa Gerbil said. "The wheel. The water bottle. But the *Mottos*? They've been around as long as we gerbils have."

"And we've been around as long as they have," said Little Gerbil. "We squeaked them!"

Grandpa thought for a moment, his tail twitching.

"You've got a point, Little Gerbil," he said. "The Mottos aren't scratched in stone, and there's no sense in good gerbils feeling bad."

"Then let's change them," she squeaked. "Just a little, so that *all* good gerbils fit."

SQUEAK BOOK

It was the most exciting Gerbil Circle since the Great Seed-Hoarding Debate.

The gerbils changed the first two Mottos.

Gerbil Mottos

The Night Is Short: Help Each Other

Keep Your Whiskers As Clean As You Can

The next two stayed the same. *Celery Tops Come To Those Who Wait* and *Many Paws Make Quick Work*—those Mottos were just facts of gerbil life.

They debated longest over *Curl Up Nose To Toes*. It was the only rhyming Motto, and gerbils have a weakness for rhymes.

"How about, *Time To Rest, Find A Nest?*" Little Gerbil finally suggested.

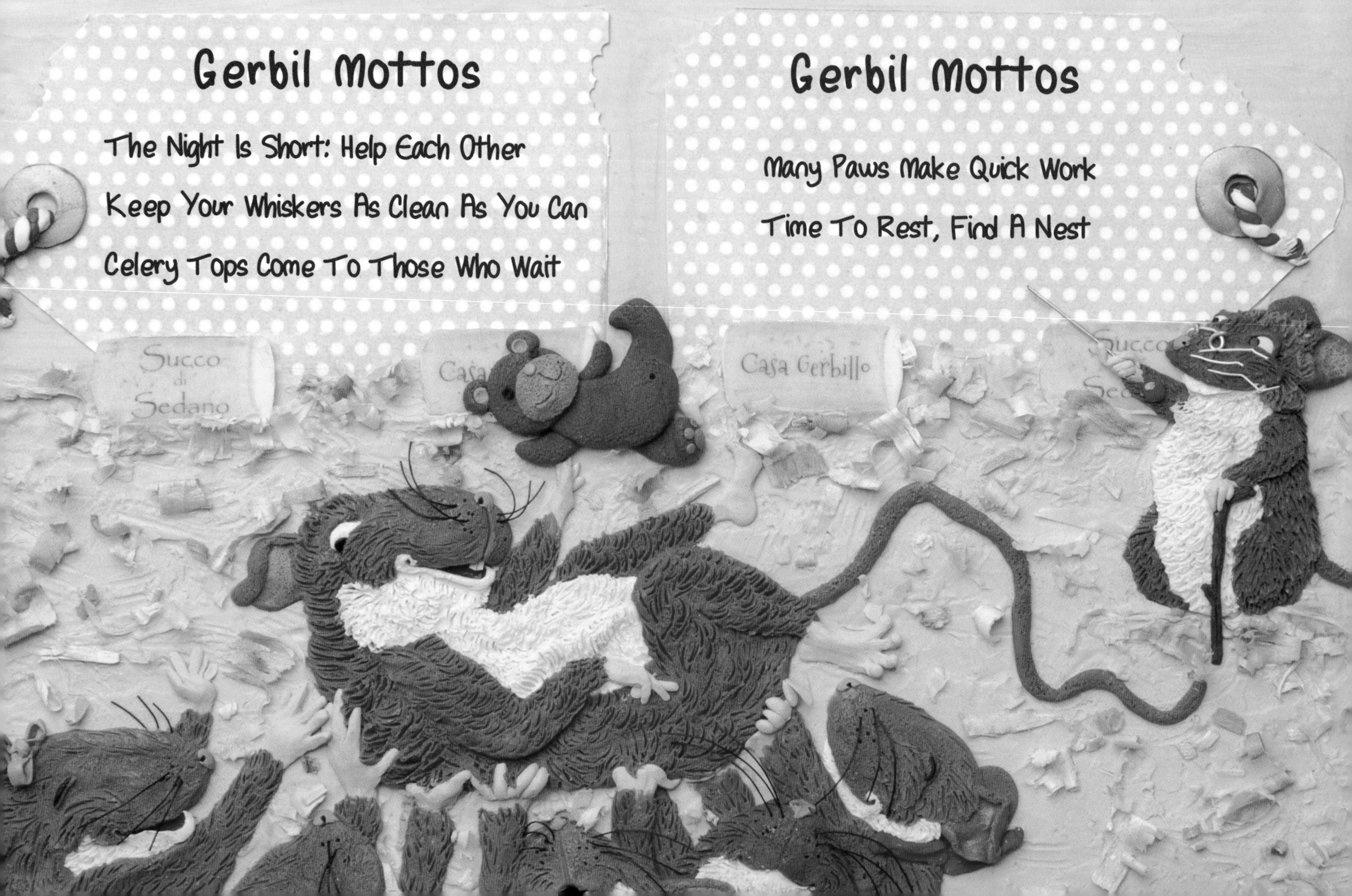

Gerbil Mottos
The Night Is Short: Help Each Other
Keep Your Whiskers As Clean As You Can
Celery Tops Come To Those Who Wait
Gerbil Mottos
Many Paws Make Quick Work
Time To Rest, Find A Nest
Succo di Sedano
Casa Gerbillo

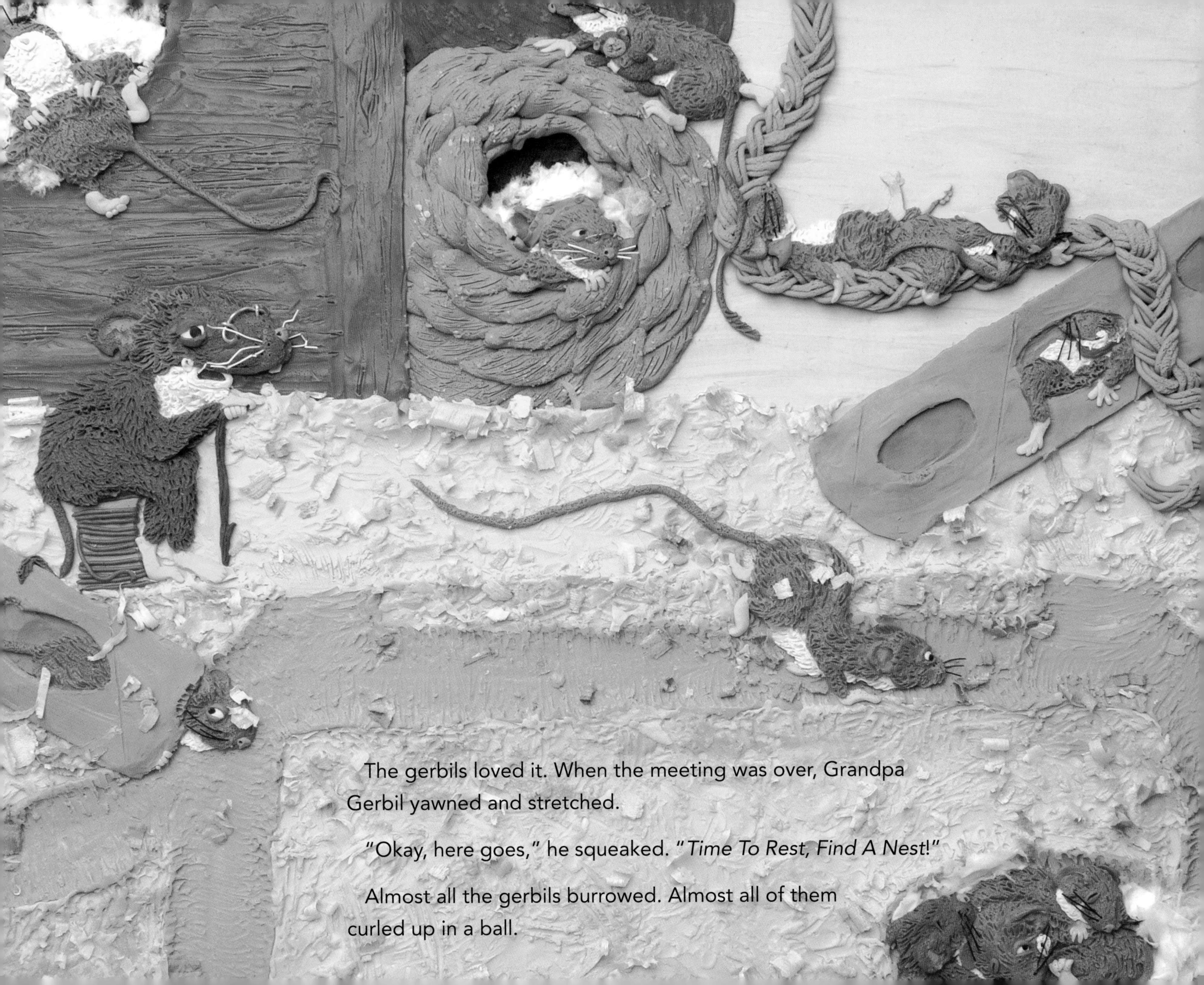

The gerbils loved it. When the meeting was over, Grandpa Gerbil yawned and stretched.

"Okay, here goes," he squeaked. "*Time To Rest, Find A Nest*!"

Almost all the gerbils burrowed. Almost all of them curled up in a ball.

But Little Gerbil scurried on top of the bedding and stretched from the tip of her nose to the ends of her toes. She smiled as she felt the sun warm her whiskers.

She was a happy gerbil, a good gerbil, uncurled.

More About Gerbils

A Rodents' Who's Who

Gerbils are rodents, a group of mammals which ranges from the tiniest African pygmy mouse (weighing less than a loonie) to the large capybara, which can reach the weight of an adult human. There are 2,277 species of rodents, including mice, squirrels, guinea pigs, rats, hamsters, beavers, and porcupines. Here's where the gerbils fit in, size-wise, with some of their relatives — other rodents people keep as house pets:

Mouse

Gerbil

Hamster

Rat

Guinea Pig

No Gerbils Allowed!

Gerbils are actually illegal in Australia and New Zealand and in the states of California and Hawaii. They are often classified as "exotic rodents" and are seen as fast-breeding threats to the local ecosystems.

Paws and Teeth

On a cold day it feels wonderful to pull the blankets over your head and burrow down into the warmth of your bed. Gerbils feel like that all the time; they have an instinctive urge to burrow and tunnel. Unlike hamsters, who appreciate ready-made tunnels, gerbils need to be able to dig their own tunnels. The best environment for gerbils is a covered aquarium with paper and aspen wood shavings.

"Rodent" is from the Latin word "rodere", which means "to gnaw". So gnawing is central to gerbil life. Along with their rodent cousins, gerbils have teeth that grow continuously, so they have to wear them down by gnawing.

The History of a House Pet

The most common kind of gerbil kept as a pet is the Mongolian Gerbil, which still lives wild in desert climates. In the late 1800s, they were brought from China to Paris, and in 1954, 40 gerbils (20 breeding pairs) were brought to the United States. Most pet gerbils today are descended from those original 40 gerbils.

Mottos—Not Only for Gerbils

Mottos are short sentences or phrases that describe the beliefs of a particular group. Some famous human mottos include: "Where there's a will, there's a way," and "Learn from yesterday; live for today; hope for tomorrow." What would your family motto be? How about your class? Your school? Your team? Your pet?

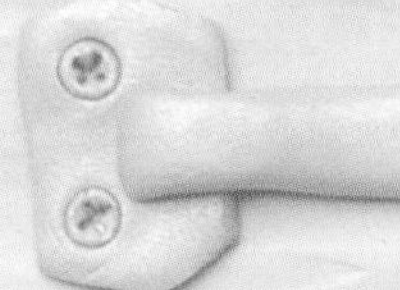

Party Animals

Gerbils are friendly, playful, social creatures that like to raise their pups and live together in family groups called clans. They do not like to live alone, and if they do, they often lead shorter, less healthy lives. If you are interested in gerbils as pets, get two females or two males; they'll be far happier. And don't mix gerbils from different clans or families. They will literally smell an intruder and may attack!

Make a Gerbil

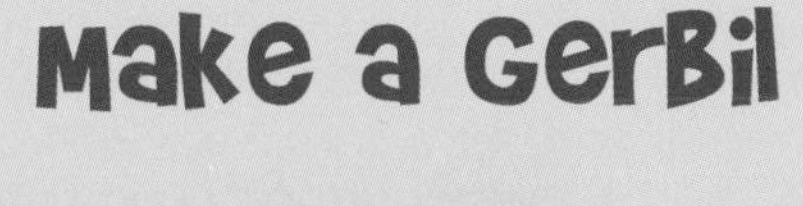

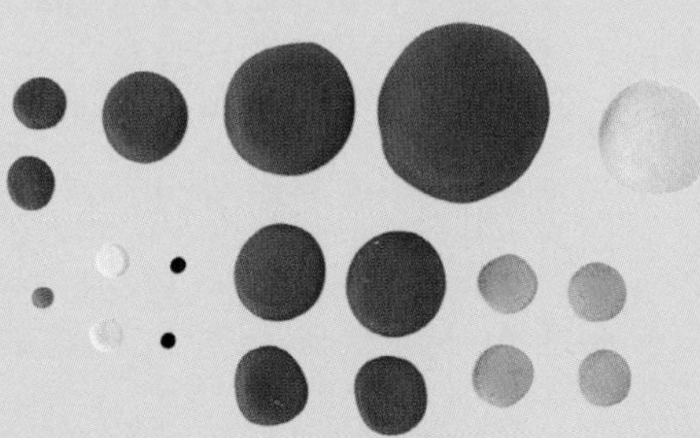

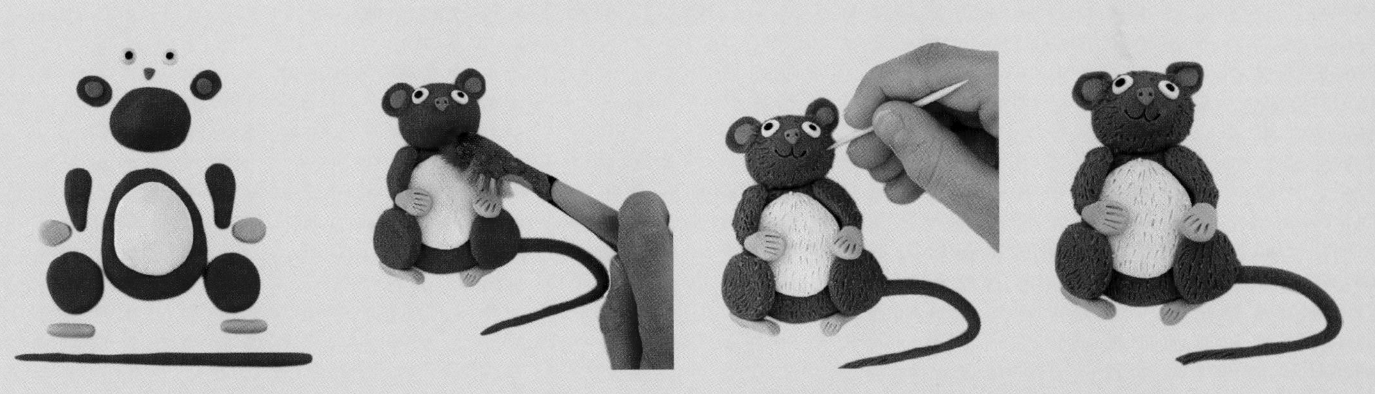

Using plasticine, roll out:

- 2 large brown balls
- 5 medium brown balls
- 2 small brown balls
- 2 small pink balls
- 1 very small pink ball
- 4 small beige balls
- 1 medium white ball
- 2 small white balls
- 2 tiny black balls

1. Use the brown balls to shape the body and head, legs, tail, and ears.
2. Flatten the large white ball to make the tummy.
3. Shape the hands and feet using the beige balls.
4. Press 2 of the pink balls onto the small brown balls to make the ears and press the tiny black balls onto the small white balls to make eyes. Shape the small pink ball into a triangle and attach for the nose.
5. Assemble all of the pieces.
6. Use an old toothbrush and toothpick to make the fur and details to the face.

The End

Gerbil Mottos

The Night Is Short: Help Each Other

Keep Your Whiskers As Clean As You Can

Celery Tops Come To Those Who Wait

Gerbil Mottos

Many Paws Make Quick Work

Time To Rest, Find A Nest